CRUISE LIFE

QUEEN of the SEA

CRUISE LIFE

QUEEN of the SEA

REESE ESCHMANN

Scholastic Inc.

ISBN 978-1-339-01815-7

10 9 8 7 6 5 4 3 2 1   25 26 27 28 29

Printed in the U.S.A.   40

First printing 2025

Book design by Cassy Price

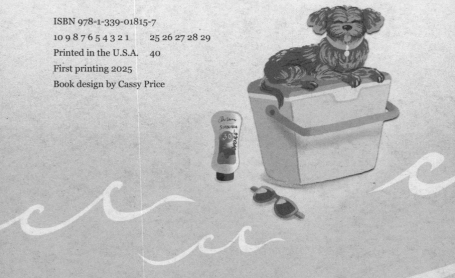

CHAPTER ONE
WHAT IF?

"Caitlin Cruz, why are there blue footprints all over my kitchen floor?"

I look at my mom's crossed arms and gulp. Crossed arms are never a good sign. I check the bottom of my feet—no blue paint there. But I was painting the ocean earlier, and I might have forgotten to put the paint away. I inspect the footprints. They're tiny and adorable. All five toes are different sizes, and at the end of each toe, I can make out a cute little claw mark.

I turn to frown at the bearded dragon sitting on my shoulder, though it's hard to be mad. I think Mom's floors look better than ever!

"Peaches," I say. "Did you walk through my paint set again? I told you, if you want to make art, you have to learn how to hold a paintbrush."

Peaches opens her mouth a little, which makes it look like she's smiling. A bearded dragon isn't like a dragon from fairy tales. Peaches doesn't breathe fire, and she can't fly. Not yet, at least.

I still think that one day, she might grow wings and fly around while red flames explode from her mouth. For now, though, Peaches spends most of her time on my shoulder, which is also covered in little blue footprints. But sometimes she gets me into trouble, like when she makes art on Mom's new floors, or sheds her extra skin on Mom's new floors, or goes to the bathroom on Mom's new floors. That only happened once.

"Sorry, Mom," I say. "I forgot to put my paint away. I'll clean it up."

Mom sighs and uncrosses her arms. "Thanks, Caitlin. I know you have a lot going on today. But I'm really trying to keep the cottage clean."

She walks out of the kitchen, leaving me and

Peaches alone. I used to live in a big, messy house with Mom, Dad, Peaches, and my older brother, Dylan. Then last year, Mom and Dad got a divorce. Now Mom lives in a little cottage by the ocean, and Dad lives in a super tall building close to the city. It's weird going back and forth between Mom's and Dad's new homes, but Peaches doesn't mind it too much.

We live near Orlando, a famous city in Florida. It's famous because there are lots of theme parks here. I think it should be famous because Peaches lives here. She's a pinkish-orange color, she's as sweet as a peach, and she has a beard made out of tiny spikes that remind me of the fuzz on a peach's skin. I think she's a lot more interesting than a roller coaster. She rubs her head against the skin below my ears and her spikes tickle my neck.

I bend down to wipe up the paint with a paper towel. While I'm cleaning, Peaches starts to shed a little bit of the skin on her cheek. It falls into the mess I'm wiping up.

"Really, Peaches? You always pick the worst times to shed." I scoop up the little pieces of Peaches's old skin. They feel rough and waxy.

"I wonder . . ." I say slowly. I pull my journal out of my back pocket. The pages are small and pocket-sized. I keep a tiny pencil tucked into the spiral holding the journal together. The cover of the journal is the same color as Peaches, and there are big words written on the front: *What If?*

Dylan wrote those words on the cover a long time ago, but he didn't write anything on the pages inside the journal. He's always doing weird stuff like that. He'll read the first chapter of a book and then forget to finish the rest. He plays the first level of a video game and then decides he doesn't want to face the final boss! Sometimes he even takes just one bite of a brownie, and then leaves the rest on his plate, looking all lonely and delicious. I like to finish things for him. Especially his brownies. But I also really love the *What If?* notebook. I use the blank pages to write down all the questions that pop into my head.

What if Peaches grew and grew until she was the size of an alligator?

What if alligator Peaches bit off
Dylan's head?

What if Dylan walked around
with no head?

I pause and write a new question.

What if I sewed together all the pieces
of Peaches's old skin?

What if I made a sail out of Peaches's
old skin and used it to make a sailboat?

I stand up on my tiptoes and look out the window in Mom's kitchen. I can see the bright blue ocean and the white foam that forms on the tops of big waves. There are lots of ships on the water. They all leave from Port Canaveral and sail up and down the coast. The big cruise ships travel all the way to islands with sparkling beaches where you can go snorkeling.

We were supposed to go on a family cruise last year. Dad said the cruise ship had an all-you-can-eat buffet, six pools, and three giant waterslides. Our trip got canceled when Mom and Dad got a divorce. But if I made a sail out of Peaches's old skin, I could join the other ships out on the water. Peaches and I could be adventurers or pirates or—

"Caitlin? Are you done cleaning up in the kitchen?" Mom's voice calls out from the living room.

"Uhh . . . almost!" I shout.

"Good, because your dad just called. He'll be here in ten minutes to pick you up! Are you ready to go?"

"Uhh . . . almost!" I say again. Peaches turns her head to one side and looks at me suspiciously. I know Peaches probably doesn't understand what I said. She's a dragon with a brain the size of a carrot. But sometimes I think she might know when I'm not telling the whole truth.

"I *am* almost done packing," I tell her. "I mean, my suitcase is open. All I have to do is dump stuff in!"

I finish wiping up the paint from the floor and throw the paper towels in the trash. Then I scoop up the little pieces of dragon skin that Peaches shed and race to my bedroom to finish packing. But not before writing one more question in the *What If?* notebook.

What if Peaches is a mega genius with a secret plan to take over the world?

I've still got a handful of dragon skin in one fist when I open the door to my bedroom.

"BOO!"

"Aaah!" I shout, stumbling backward. Dragon skin goes flying everywhere. My brother, Dylan, was hiding behind my door waiting to scare me. He's pointing his phone at me and laughing. We like to take videos of ourselves scaring each other. One day, we'll edit all the videos together and make a scary movie. I bet this video will be a good one—I really didn't think Dylan was going to be in my room!

I push my eyebrows together and pretend to be mad. "Dylan, your brain is even smaller than a carrot! What are you doing in my room?"

"Man, Peaches's dragon skin went *everywhere*. That was awesome." Dylan turns off the video and bends over to help me pick up some of the pieces from the floor.

"We're going to be sharing a room at Dad's place all summer," he says. He plops down on my bed. "You need to get used to me being around every corner. Get ready for the scariest summer of your life."

I grab a container of crickets and shake them in front of Dylan's face.

"Ugh, get those away from me," he says, making a horrified face. He's mostly pretending, but I know a part of him is actually scared of bugs. I saw him run from a spider once.

"They're Peaches's favorite snack," I say. "If we're going to share a room for six weeks, then *you* need to get used to having bugs around."

Usually, when we go to Dad's house for the weekend, Dylan sleeps on the couch in the living room, and I sleep in the extra bedroom. But this time, we're staying at Dad's condo for six whole weeks! Instead of spending weekdays with Mom and weekends with Dad, we'll spend six weeks with Dad, then six weeks with Mom. I'm glad

Peaches and I won't have to travel back and forth for a while. And Dylan and I are going to get so much time to creep each other out.

Dylan looks a little bit more like Dad, with light brown skin and almost-straight black hair. I look more like Mom—with skin that she calls rich brown and a head full of shiny curls. Thinking of my curls reminds me to pack my sleep bonnet, comb, and curly hair cream. Mom's been teaching me how to do my hair so I can help Dad, who's still figuring it out.

I throw the container of crickets into my suitcase, along with a pile of shorts and T-shirts. I also pack my adventure boots and the little harness that Peaches wears when we go on walks outside. On my shoulder, Peaches nods approvingly. She loves going on adventures, just like me!

Just then, I hear Dad's voice in the hallway. Dylan and I run out to greet him. He's wearing his blue scrubs, which means he's coming from a shift at the hospital.

"Hey, Dad!" I say. I give him a hug, and he gives Peaches a little pat on the head. "I'm almost all the way packed for the summer."

Dad and Mom exchange a look, and Mom laughs.

"Well . . . I hope you have some room left in your suitcase," Dad says. "Because I have a big announcement!"

Dylan scrunches up his face in confusion, and Peaches tilts her head to the side again.

"Pack extra swimsuits and sunscreen because I got a summer job as a cruise ship doctor! The cruise leaves today and you two are coming with me—as long as you don't mind spending a week on a boat with six pools, three waterslides, and unlimited ice cream!"

Peaches's mouth drops open in shock. I can't believe it either. No more *what-if*s. I'm going on a cruise—for real!

CHAPTER TWO
YO-YOS & TIPPY TAPS

My heart bounces up and down in my chest like a yo-yo. One second, I feel so excited I can hardly breathe, and then the next second, my heart plummets down into my stomach and makes me feel heavy.

"Does that mean we won't be staying at your house for six weeks?" I ask. My voice trembles a little.

Dad runs his hand through his dark, shaggy hair. He always does that when he's worried. "Well, the schedule will have to change a little bit. Your mom and I have been working on a new plan. But I thought you'd be excited. You've always wanted to go on a cruise!"

My heart bounces back up into my throat. I can't think of anything to say.

Dylan's shoulder brushes against mine. "A cruise sounds cool, but Caitlin and I were excited about spending a lot of time in one place. We've even been getting used to sharing a room."

I sigh in relief. Dylan said all the words I couldn't. Sometimes he acts like a bossy big brother, and sometimes he acts like a dragon with a brain the size of a carrot, but mostly he acts like my best friend. Thinking about Dylan's carrot brain reminds me of something else.

"And what about Peaches? I can't leave her behind!"

Dad smiles. "I got permission for Peaches to join us! This is a pet-friendly cruise ship. They even have special cruises sometimes where every-one onboard brings an animal! I think Peaches will love it."

My heart yo-yo slows down. I imagine Peaches chilling by the side of a pool wearing tiny dragon sunglasses. She'd love crunching on the veggies at the all-you-can-eat salad bar! I turn to Dylan. He's looking at me, waiting to see how I feel about this new information. I smile, and he smiles back.

"So, I should probably pack some of my cruisin' fits, right?" he asks. Dylan says *fits* instead of *outfits* because he thinks that's how teenagers talk, but he still has two whole years before he turns thirteen!

"Definitely," Dad says. "Bring all your summer gear. And I promise, your mom and I will make sure you both get lots of time in one place with each of us."

Mom nods in agreement. "We'll let you know the plan as soon as we finish working out our schedules. We love you both so much. You're going to have an amazing time!"

Dylan and I race back to our bedrooms to finish packing. I put Peaches in her tank. Then I throw all my swimsuits, a big sun hat, and flip-flops into my bag, along with other essentials like 3D glasses and a tiny shirt with butterfly wings that Grandma made for Peaches. I even pack my princess dresses and some Halloween costumes— you never know what kind of parties they'll have on a cruise! Peaches's claws *tip tap* against the glass of her tank. I love when she gets the tippy taps! It means she's excited. Dad carefully carries her huge tank out to the car and puts it on a blanket in the back seat.

I give Mom a huge goodbye hug, then I sit next to Peaches. I keep my hand on top of her tank while we drive. Dad drives along the beach road that will take us to Port Canaveral. Dylan rolls down the window in the front seat and sticks his arm out, letting it float up and down as he talks about the cruise.

"Alright, Dad, here's my schedule for the first day. At seven a.m. I'll wake up, eat a big plate of eggs, and then hit the cruise gym. Then I'll crush some bacon strips and swim laps in the biggest pool. By the end of the week, I'll be so beefy, you won't even recognize me!"

He lifts his arm and kisses the spot where muscles would be if he had any. Knowing Dylan, he'll eat a big plate of eggs and then go back to bed for another three hours. Which sounds great to me! Peaches and I love naps. I can't believe we get to spend a whole week relaxing on a cruise ship!

I lean my head against the window as we drive. Dylan and Dad are still talking about their plans. I let their voices fade into the background and look out at all the people on the beach. There's a very fancy-looking lady walking on the beach in high heels. Two men dressed in black walk behind her. Maybe she's a famous actress and those are her bodyguards! I also see a family building a sand-castle that's almost as tall as me, a woman wearing something that looks like a white snowsuit, and two kids with blue mohawks. I wish I could talk to all those people and find out their stories and their *what-if*s.

There will be so many interesting people on the cruise. I can't wait to talk to them! I let my brain go quiet and listen to Dad and Dylan. Dad is telling us what we'll be doing on the cruise while he's working.

"All the staff on the cruise ship are supposed to help the guests have a great stay. That includes you two. So I want to make sure you follow the cruise ship rules and offer help to anyone who needs it."

I sit up straight. "I can help! I'll swim in every pool. That way, I'll know where all the pools are and which water is the warmest. Then I can help people find their way!"

"That's a great idea, Caitlin," Dad says.

"Caitlin and I have this in the bag, Dad," Dylan says. "We've been helping out lost tourists since we were babies. That's the price of being an Orlando kid."

He sighs and shrugs his shoulders like he's an old man talking about the hard life he's lived. But I know he loves Orlando as much as I do.

Dad turns onto a road taking us down to the docks at Port Canaveral.

"Well, there she is," he says. We pull up in front of a huge cruise ship with a clean white hull that shines in the sun. I count at least seven floors with circular windows and balconies. On top of the ship, I see the three waterslides. One is yellow, one is blue, and the biggest one is clear—it wraps all the way around the top of the cruise ship. There are swirly purple letters printed on the back of the ship.

"'The Wandering Princess,'" I read out loud. "Who is she?"

Dad smiles. "Let's go find out."

CHAPTER THREE

ALL ABOARD!

I'm pretty sure Rule #1 of cruise life is *Don't run on deck*, but that doesn't make it any easier to keep my pace slow. Dad leads us up a wide ramp onto the ship. I zigzag my way up, tapping the railings on both sides as I go. I can't wait to see *everything*!

The ramp leads us into a fancy-looking lobby. It looks like a hotel, with clean white walls and blue diamond patterns printed on the carpet. I can't even tell that we're on the water! The ship is so big that it doesn't rock with the waves. It feels safe and steady, just like a house.

Dad leads us into an elevator on the other side of the lobby. There's a sign above the elevator buttons telling us what's on every floor. There are eleven whole floors on the cruise ship! One floor is labeled B—STAFF ONLY, and after that the rest of the floors are numbered 1 through 10. That's a *lot* of space to explore. Before I can stop myself, I reach out to push the button for FLOOR #9—*MAIN POOL*, but Dad clears his throat.

He raises an eyebrow at me. He's carrying three bags on his shoulders. Sweat drips down his face as he struggles to hold Peaches's giant tank.

"Dad, have you been staying hydrated?" I ask him. "You look tired."

The nice thing about having a doctor as a dad is that he always gives me tips about how to make sure I'm feeling my best. Drinking water is one of those things.

Dad grimaces. "I'll drink some water as soon as we get to our rooms."

I sigh. "Okay. I guess we should drop our bags off before we go to the pool."

"Push the button for the lower level," Dad says.

Dylan and I both jump for it, but he reaches the button before I do. We step inside the elevator, and Dylan rattles off some of the other ship attractions listed on the floor guide. "Arcade, cafeteria, hot tub, sauna . . . this is AWESOME!"

The elevator dings as we reach the lower level of the cruise ship—the one labeled B.

"This is where we're going to live this week!" Dad says. His voice sounds a little strained from all the stuff he's carrying, but I can tell he's excited. "Only staff are allowed down here. The guests stay on the other floors."

I smile. We get to live in a secret ship basement. Maybe Peaches and I will become spies!

The elevator door opens. There's an important-looking lady standing outside, holding a clipboard. She's older than Mom but younger than Grandma. There are a few strands of gray hair in her curly 'fro.

"Dr. Cruz!" she says with a big smile on her face. "Welcome! This must be your beautiful family."

She leans in and presses her nose to the glass on Peaches's tank. "I've heard a lot about this lady. Can't wait to have her onboard! You know, I'm the one who pushed for the *Wandering Princess* to be a pet-friendly cruise. I just *love* all animals!"

I smile back at her.

"Plus, your dad promised me that you have the most well-behaved bearded dragon in the world. I'm sure there won't be any issues with your lizard onboard."

I gulp and run my hands down my shirt to make sure there aren't any stray bits of Peaches's skin stuck to it.

"Kids, this is Simone," Dad says. "She's the cruise ship manager! You have her to thank for my job and all the amenities you'll get to enjoy while you're here!"

"Thank you so much," I say in my most polite voice. "We're really excited to help the guests however we can. My brother, Dylan, is very good at making plans, which I'm sure will come in handy. And I have excellent people skills."

Dylan raises an eyebrow at me. I shrug. The first step in becoming really good at something is telling everyone how good you are at it. That's what happened last summer when Dylan told us all he was a pro skateboarder. At first, he came home every day with scrapes on his knees. But by the end of the summer, he could do a flip on his skateboard! So if I tell everyone I'm a people person, I'm sure I'll become one.

Simone nods approvingly. "Excellent. We're excited to have you here. Your cabins are three doors down on the left, across from the Leone family."

Simone hands Dad our keys. They open the doors to two rooms that are connected by a bathroom. Dad has his own room and bed. Dylan and I have bunk beds in our room!

"Sweet!" he shouts. "We've never had bunk beds before. You want the top or bottom?"

"Hmm . . ." I start to think. I wish I could make a pros and cons list in my *What If?* notebook, but there's no time for that now. Dylan and I have a lot of exploring to do as soon as we get unpacked. I think fast.

"Well, Dad said a good spot for Peaches's tank is in the corner, by the outlets. If I sleep on the bottom bunk, then my head will be right next to Peaches! I'll be able to plug in my night-light *and* her heater lights. That sounds nice. Also I don't want to fall out of bed."

"I don't mind falling out," Dylan says, scrambling to the top bunk. "I have a really strong skull, so I'll be okay if I hit my head."

We unpack our stuff, and I give Peaches a few crickets. Dad said not to take her exploring on the first day. She needs time to get settled in her new home! I plug in the heat bulbs that stretch across the top of the tank. Peaches loves getting nice and warm under the lights while she climbs on her rocks and nibbles lettuce.

"See you soon, Peaches!" I say.

Dylan knocks on the door that connects to

Dad's room. Dad comes inside to inspect our room. He nods approvingly.

"Wow, you unpacked fast!" Dad says. He hands us each a key to the room. *Whoa*. I've never had my own key before. I zip it into a secret pocket in my shorts. I don't want to lose it and make Dad think I don't belong on the ship.

"Okay," Dad continues. "You can explore the ship for one hour. Remember to walk slowly and take your time. And be sure to introduce your-selves to anyone you see. The cruise guests don't get here until later tonight, so everyone onboard right now is one of the staff! I'm going to head to the infirmary to get my equipment set up."

Dad leaves, then Dylan starts filming every corner of our room so he can tell Mom what we're up to. When he's ready to go, I double-check that I have my room key and my *What If?* notebook. As soon as we step out of our cabin, we run into some of the other staff in the hallway. And they're kids, just like us! They look exactly the same, except one has hair and one does not. The bald one smiles at me.

"Hey, I'm Max," he says. "This is Olivia. We're twins."

Olivia stretches out her hand, and I shake it, feeling very grown-up. "If you're wondering why Max has no hair, don't bother asking," she says. "He won't tell you. It's too embarrassing."

I wasn't going to ask, but now my mind starts racing with all the things that might have happened to Max's hair. Maybe he fell in a tub of hair-dissolving acid! Or it got dusty, and a vacuum sucked it straight out of his head, but forgot to take his eyebrows.

"I think it looks cool," Dylan says. "I'm Dylan, and this is my little sis, Caitlin."

"Is this your first time on the *Wandering Princess*?" Olivia asks.

"It's our first time on *any* cruise ship!" I say.

"Ah, I remember my first cruise," Max says. "Those were good times." He sighs and looks down the hallway as though he's remembering something that happened a long, long time ago.

"This is our second summer doing the cruise circuit with our grandpa," Olivia says. "His name is Chef Benedict Leone. He's cooked for people in more than twenty countries all over the world! But he says cooking for this many people at once is his biggest challenge yet."

"How many people are gonna be on the cruise?" Dylan asks.

"A few thousand," Olivia says.

"Actually, the cruise ship manifest says there are going to be 3,026 passengers on this trip!" Max says. "That's more than three times the amount of kids that go to our school."

Olivia shoots Max a stern look. "I know. I saw

the passenger list too. But I didn't want to scare the newbies off with such a big number."

I don't even have time to wonder what a *newbie* is. My brain is too busy trying to imagine 3,026 people in one place.

"Whoa," I say. "Are we going to meet all of them?"

"Of course not," Olivia says. "Grandpa always tells us to help the guests, but three thousand people is too many to keep up with!"

"Plus, people on vacation have a lot of demands!" Max says. "Don't worry, I know all the best spots to hide from passengers who ask too many questions."

Max really seems like he knows what he's talking about. Dad always says bald people are wise. But this ship is supposed to be our home too! I don't want Max to think we don't belong.

"That's okay," I say. "This might be our first cruise, but Dylan and I have lived in Florida our whole lives. We know a lot about helping tourists."

"Yeah, we're not exactly newbies," Dylan says. He's standing up tall and his chest is puffed a bit. I think he wants to seem as important as Max and Olivia. I do too! I still don't know what a newbie is, but I don't think I want to be one.

"That's good," Olivia says. "But I wish people knew that when you're on vacation you're supposed to chill out by the pool, not keep asking for extra ice cubes in your soda!"

I make a face. "I don't even like ice cubes. They hurt my brain."

"Same," says Max.

"Is that what happened to your hair?" I ask him. "Ice cubes froze it off?"

Max's mouth straightens into a line. He shakes his head seriously.

"I told you," Olivia says, rolling her eyes. "He won't talk about it. Come on, let's go get some food."

Max enters the elevator and immediately pushes the button for the fourth floor. He doesn't even have to look at the sign to know where he's going. I double-check it, and see that Max was right. Floor #4 is where the cafeteria is.

"How do you know where everything is?" I ask. "This ship is so big!"

"I make a map whenever I board a new ship," he says. "It's no big deal. You newbies will learn soon enough. Wanna see it?"

He pulls a folded piece of paper from his pocket and hands it to Dylan.

Dylan unfolds it. His eyes get wide. "Whoa, this makes this place seem even bigger and more awesome than the view from the dock!"

"Yeah," Max says. "All the coolest stuff is at the front of the ship. There are seven floors of cabins at the back—that's where all the passengers stay. One thousand five hundred rooms for guests! That's a lot of bathrooms to clean. It's hard work to keep such a big ship running."

"Max, you've never cleaned a bathroom in your life," Olivia says. "Not even your own."

"I never said I cleaned them," Max protests. "I just said it's hard work, which is true."

Olivia rolls her eyes.

I peek over Dylan's shoulder to get a look at the map. There are so many floors packed with cool things, and Max labeled all the most important places.

Whoa. I still can't believe we're here. This ship is my new home. I decide I'm going to learn as

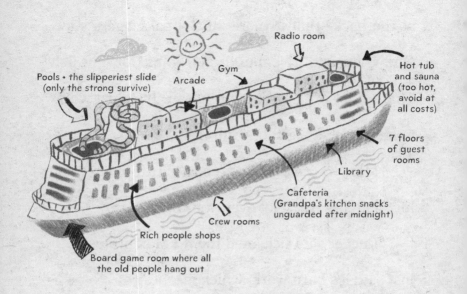

Radio room

Gym

Arcade

Pools + the slipperiest slide
(only the strong survive)

Hot tub
and sauna
(too hot,
avoid at
all costs)

7 floors
of guest
rooms

Library

Cafeteria
(Grandpa's kitchen snacks
unguarded after midnight)

Crew rooms

Rich people shops

Board game room where all
the old people hang out

much about it as Max. That way the *Wandering Princess* will love me as much as I love her.

The elevator dings as we reach the fourth floor. Max and Olivia step out, but I grab Dylan's sleeve, holding him back.

"Dylan," I whisper. "What's a newbie? Is it the same as a noogie?"

"A newbie just means you're new at something. This is our first cruise, so we don't know as much as those other two. We've got a lot of work to do to become expert crew kids."

Dylan stops when he sees the frown on my face. "But we'll learn. Don't worry. And *this* is a noogie."

He pulls me in and rubs his knuckles against the top of my head, mushing my curls into my skull.

"Urgh, get off me! I'm telling Mom it's your fault when she asks why my hair is so tangled."

Dylan laughs, then stops and flares his nostrils. "Mmm. You smell that?"

I breathe in deep through my nose, then step out of the elevator like I'm in a trance. It smells *amazing* in the dining hall. I wave my hand in front of my face. I want to bring more of these delicious smells over to my nose, like a fancy person at an even fancier restaurant who's about to tell you all the ingredients in their pasta.

Max and Olivia are a few feet ahead playing some kind of game where they flick each other on the nose. They stop when they see me, and start waving smells toward their own noses. Dylan does the same.

"Ooh, is that a hint of rosemary?" Dylan asks in a British accent.

"I do believe I've caught a whiff of tuna!" Olivia says.

"Oh my! Can it be? Is that . . . fresh mint I'm smelling?" Max coos.

I try not to laugh. I press my lips together, then speak in my most high-pitched, fancy-pants voice. "Well, I'll say! It smells like a French *pat-ee-ser-oo* in here."

Dylan, Max, and Olivia turn their heads to look at me. I giggle. "I forgot what those places with the croissants are called."

Olivia smiles and puts her arm around me. "It's *patisserie*. But I like your version better."

I smile back. I think this means Olivia and I are friends now. Olivia is really nice, and she doesn't call us newbies. Maybe that's because she's trying to get on my good side. Turns out I *do* have excellent people skills! I imagine living on the ship all summer with the Leone family. It would be nice for me and Dylan to have friends we could talk to every day. We just have to become expert crew kids like them, then we'll fit right in with Max too.

"Let's sit over there by the big window," Max says. "Best seats in the house."

He leads us to a big table in the corner of the room. The whole room is filled with hundreds of tables covered in clean white tablecloths. Some of the tables are long and look like they could seat at least twenty people! Other tables are smaller and shaped like circles. Three of the walls in the dining hall are covered in colorful paintings of different fruits and vegetables. The painting of a peach makes my mouth water. I want to bite right into it! The fourth wall is made entirely of windows that show us the blue ocean and the other ships docked at Port Canaveral.

The table Max leads us to is right next to the window. It's also right next to the start of a super long table covered in large silver platters. It's the buffet line! This *is* the best table in the hall, except there's not any food out yet.

"All those smells mean Grandpa's cooking in the kitchen," Olivia says. "I bet he's working on welcome snacks for when the guests arrive later. They must not be ready yet!"

Max grabs the sides of his head in frustration.

I think he would be pulling out his hair, if he had any.

I set my notebook on the table. Maybe I can make a list of *what-if*s about Max's hair. If I show it to him, he might give me a clue about what happened. He can't call me a newbie once I discover the secret of his baldness. But before I can start writing, the smell of fresh brownies fills my nostrils. Olivia and Max sit up straight.

"Quadruple chocolate chip," Olivia says. "Grandpa's favorite."

Now I feel like I'm in one of those cartoons where you can actually *see* smells. I stand up and walk toward the brownie smell, imagining a purple cloud in front of me, leading the way.

A man with white hair and a white chef's hat walks out of a door behind the buffet line. He's carrying a giant platter filled with more brownies than I can count.

"Chef Benedict?" I say. "Hi. I'm Caitlin. I didn't even know there *were* four types of chocolate."

"Then you've got to try one of these brownies," he says. He smiles at Max and Olivia. "I'm glad you two are making friends and staying out of trouble."

Max and Olivia smirk at each other.

"Don't worry, Chef," I say. "My dad is the ship doctor, so if they do get into trouble, I'll be able to help patch them up! But I don't know how to regrow hair overnight. I don't think my dad does either."

Chef Benedict laughs. He lifts up his chef's hat

to reveal that the top of his head is bald too. "That would be nice if he did, eh? But I'd choose quadruple chocolate brownies over hair any day."

"Me too," Olivia, Max, and I say at the same time. We each grab a brownie, and I grab an extra one for Dylan, who stayed at the table.

I can't help eating my whole brownie in one bite. It's warm and gooey, and all the chocolate flavors make me want to dance.

At the table, Dylan has my notebook opened to a blank page. Or at least, it was a blank page before he started scribbling on it.

"Hey!" I protest. "What are you writing in my notebook?"

He slides the notebook over to me. I read his

handwriting, which is very messy, but also much neater than my handwriting.

The Perfect Plan: Cruise Day One

7 a.m.: All-you-can-eat buffet

8 a.m.: Swim laps in the pool

9 a.m.: Take Peaches to the sauna

I frown. "Dylan, you took up a whole page in my notebook and you didn't even finish the schedule. You never finish anything!"

Dylan shrugs. "I might finish this brownie. It's the best one I've ever had."

"Who's Peaches?" Olivia asks. She's reading Dylan's schedule over my shoulder.

"Peaches is my pet dragon."

"Wait, you have a DRAGON?" Max shouts.

"Yes, but she's a bearded dragon. She doesn't breathe fire. Yet."

Olivia's and Max's big eyes bulge in excitement. They start to speak over each other, and I can't understand what they're saying. They realize what they're doing and stop. Then they speak at the same time.

"We need to meet this dragon. Right. NOW!"

Dylan chews the last bite of his brownie. "She'd love to meet you, but you should know that she eats bugs."

"What!" Max exclaims. "I mean, of course I knew that pets were allowed on the ship, but I've only ever seen spoiled dogs onboard. A bug-eating dragon is *awesome*."

We take the elevator back down to the lower level. Max and Olivia are so excited that I start to get worried that they'll spook Peaches. But as soon as we get inside our room, they speak in quiet voices and move slowly toward the tank.

"Our cat had babies once," Olivia says. "So we know how to be gentle with animals."

That makes me feel really good. I take Peaches out of her tank and let her crawl around the room. Max and Olivia take turns gently touching her spikes. Then they feed her some crickets. I think Peaches is as happy to have new friends as I am!

"Where's your cat now?" I ask.

"She's with our neighbor back at home in Indiana," Olivia says. "Our parents have to go on long trips in other countries for work. That's why we do the cruise circuit with Grandpa."

She pauses and looks a little embarrassed. "It's kind of a weird life, I guess. Most of our other friends just stay in one place all year."

"Dylan and I don't think it's weird," I say. I give her a comforting smile—the kind a people person would give.

"Yeah, our parents are divorced, so we move between homes a lot too," Dylan says.

Max leans back on the floor, puts his hands behind his head, and sighs happily. "As soon as you two learn the ropes of the ship, you'll feel right at home. I don't miss Indiana at all. Nothing is better than life at sea!"

I furrow my brows together. *Learn the ropes?* I'm not sure what that means. Dylan and I are going to have to figure out how to get around all ten floors of this place, *and* we're going to have to learn how to tie some ropes? Maybe we need to know special knots to tie all the floaties in the pool together. I'm a little clumsy, and Peaches's claws can shred ropes, but hopefully we'll figure it out.

Dad opens the door to our room. He raises an eyebrow when he sees Dylan and I aren't alone.

"Dad, these are Chef Benedict's grandkids,"

Dylan says. "Max and Olivia. This is like their hundredth cruise."

Dad smiles. "Nice to meet you. Thanks for showing my kids what's what. Just wanted to let you all know that the guests are about to arrive."

My heart thumps fast. I pick up Peaches and hold her close to my chest. I'm not sure I'm ready for the passengers to arrive. I still have so many ropes to learn. Peaches and I haven't had enough time to settle into our new home. She hasn't even gone exploring yet!

"You ready, Caitlin?" Dylan asks. He looks excited. I bet he's thinking about his perfect cruise day plan. I don't know why he's not as nervous about our new home as I am. Then I see that Max and Olivia are looking at me too. I don't want to seem like a newbie, so I put on my biggest *people person* smile.

"I've never been more ready," I say. "Let's go greet the guests."

CHAPTER FOUR

TRAGIC TALES

I put Peaches's harness and leash on, and she scuttles across the floor as we head back up to the lobby. While we're in the elevator, I loop the end of Peaches's leash around my wrist so my hand is free to write in my journal. I might not have a map like Max's, but there are other ways to learn more about the ship! I copy the floor descriptions from the sign.

Floor B—Staff Only

Floor #1—Lobby, help desk

Floor #2—Casino, board games

Floor #3—Shops, library

Floor #4—Dining hall

Floor #5—Auditorium, infirmary

Floor #6—Gym, indoor pool

Floor #7—Sauna, hot tubs

Floor #8—Arcade

Floor #9—Main pool

Floor #10—Upper deck, radio tower

My handwriting gets messier as I rush to scribble it all down before we get to the lobby. At the bottom, I add one more line.

What if I never learn my way around, and Peaches and I get lost onboard forever?

"Are you a writer?" Olivia asks as we reach the lobby. She smiles and waves at passengers coming onboard the ship as we talk, so I do the same.

"Um, kind of," I say. "I love to ask questions. What about you?"

"That's cool," Olivia says. "I'm not a writer, but I love reading. My whole suitcase is full of books! I can't wait to sit by the pool tomorrow and read."

"I won't have time for sitting," Dylan says. "I've got a plan! I can't wait to hit the gym, the buffet, and the slides."

"*If* you can handle the slides," Max says. "The big one is pretty intense. All the crew members rode it yesterday. It's kind of like a ritual they all do before a new cruise. But even some of the adults were scared. I did it three times though."

He smirks, and Olivia rolls her eyes.

I gulp. I've been so excited for the slides, but I didn't know they were going to be scary!

"Did you go on the biggest slide?" I ask Olivia.

She shrugs. "I did it once. Like Max said, it *is* kind of a ritual. Everyone does it."

"Yeah, I'm sure it'll be fun," I say. "Peaches might not go on it though. She doesn't like slipping around."

We keep waving at the passengers until our arms get tired. It's pretty fun though. Some of them stop to tell me how cute Peaches is. And a few of them ask for directions to their rooms. Max and Olivia help them out. I wish I knew as much as them. As the last passengers arrive, my stomach starts to grumble.

"We can't eat dinner until after the passengers eat," Max says. "But there are snacks in the arcade room. I'll show you."

"The arcade is on Floor Eight!" I say.

Max nods approvingly at me. "Nice one. You're learning the ropes already."

I puff out my chest with pride. "I'll be an expert soon. You'll see."

We ride the elevator up to the eighth floor. It opens up to a huge arcade with a blue carpet and red walls. There are rows and rows of games with blinking lights and colorful banners. I see a few of my favorites: air hockey, basketball, and life-sized *Fruit Ninja*. Peaches waddles over the carpet happily. Max shows us where to get chips and granola bars, and passes out some crew cards we can use to play the games for free. I put Peaches on my shoulder while I shoot hoops into a basket that moves up and down. For a while, all I can hear are the chimes of the games and Dylan's cackles as he beats Max in air hockey. Then a loud buzzing sound interrupts us, coming from loudspeakers overhead.

I set my basketball down and head over to Olivia. She's sitting on the motorcycle of a racing game, but she's not actually playing—she's reading one of her books! She looks up when Simone's voice replaces the buzzing sound.

"Ooh, I love this," she says. "Every night on the ship, Simone tells the story of the wandering princess."

"Wait, does that mean—" I start, but Olivia puts her finger over her lips and closes her book.

Peaches and I sit on one of the motorcycles next to her and listen to Simone's voice.

"—So pleased to have you all onboard. We hope that this week will exceed all your expectations. I'm looking forward to clear skies and bright blue waves as we all brave the seas together. As is the tradition aboard this ship, I'd like to tell you the legend of the wandering princess. There are some who say the spirit of the princess is still onboard the ship. It's what inspires us and fills our hearts with joy while we're on our journey."

My eyes open wide. I smile at Olivia.

Simone continues, "Legend has it, the first sailors on this ship docked one day on a deserted island. There, they found a princess who couldn't remember where she was from. But she was beautiful, and she wore a crown made entirely of emeralds. The sailors promised to protect her and find her kingdom. She wandered from country to country onboard the ship, but no one the sailors encountered had heard of her or her emerald crown. Time passed, and different crews of sailors came and went, but the princess never found where she belonged. Near the end of her life, she gave up her search and accepted that she wasn't a princess. After all, a princess without a kingdom is just a girl. She left the ship, and now she wanders the skies, traveling alongside shooting stars, always looking for a home that can't be found. But her spirit remains here with us, and we remember her journey as we sail the seas together. Myself and my crew are your sailors, and we hope that all our guests will feel like royalty this week. Be sure to ask for our special wandering princess hot stone massage in the spa. Good night."

I let out a deep breath as the loudspeaker switches off.

"What do you think?" Olivia asks. "I like to imagine the princess here with us, and in the stars! You can see them so clearly from the upper deck at night."

"I liked the story," I say. "But it's so sad. I wish the princess had found her home."

Olivia shrugs. "If she had, then she wouldn't

still be here with us. I love tragic stories. I'm read-ing another one right now! Want to see?"

She shows me her book. The title reads *Where the Red Fern Grows.*

"That's okay," I say. "I think Peaches is ready for dinner. And then bed. It's been a long day."

But our week has just begun.

CHAPTER FIVE

PEACHES IN LOVE

I open my eyes, sit up straight, and almost hit my head on the upper bunk.

"Caitlin? You okay?" Dylan's sleepy voice asks.

"Yeah, I was just dreaming about the wandering princess," I say. In my dream, she was haunting the ship. She couldn't remember what floor the dining hall was on, so she went around scaring people hoping they'd drop their granola bars.

"What time is it?" Dylan asks. I look at the clock on my night-light.

"Nine twenty-three."

"WHAT? We're already two hours and twenty-three minutes behind our plan!"

Dylan jumps down from the top bunk and races into the bathroom to brush his teeth. I wait behind the bathroom door for him while holding my phone. It's his turn to get totally scared by me. When he runs out of the bathroom, I jump on his back and shout, "BOO!"

"Aaaah!" Dylan shouts. He sprays my phone with minty-fresh slobber.

"Ugh, gross! I was going to send that video to Mom," I say.

"We don't have time for scary videos today, Caitlin!" Dylan says. "We're already so late."

I should tell him to slow down—especially because he has his shirt on backward—but I'm excited for our first full day on the cruise ship too! I won't be like the wandering princess in my dream. I'm going to learn where everything is and become a crew kid expert like Max! I get myself and Peaches ready and wipe the slob off my phone. Dad left us a note on the door that said he's gone to work in the ship infirmary on Floor #5. He reminds us to be careful and helpful, and to keep Peaches on her leash.

Dylan and I head to the dining hall first and are greeted by the smells of sizzling bacon and make-your-own waffles. There are guests at almost every table! But I see Chef Benedict standing by the omelet station, and Max and Olivia at the table we were at yesterday.

I pile my plate high with biscuits, bacon, and some lettuce and bell peppers. They're for Peaches. I would *never* eat vegetables for breakfast.

Once we have enough food to feed eight Caitlins and six bearded dragons, Dylan and I join Max and Olivia at their table.

"I can't believe you guys slept so long!" Max says. "I was up hours ago. I've been helping lost passengers all morning." I wonder if he ever sleeps. Maybe that's why he has no hair. He doesn't get his beauty rest.

"I know!" Dylan says. "We're way behind our schedule! We're going to have to make up for lost time."

I want to remind him that it's still early in the day, but I'm sure it won't help. He's already shoving a waffle the size of his face into his mouth.

Two minutes later, he tells me and Peaches to pack up our plates. Peaches looks offended. She was really enjoying her bell peppers. I don't like feeling rushed either. Dylan and I finally get to spend a whole week in one place. We should be relaxing!

"Just bring your plates with you," Dylan says. "We can keep eating while we're at the arcade. I want to get there before it gets too crowded."

"People on cruise ships do love to snack everywhere. Maybe I'll make an extra plate to take with me too," Olivia says.

We load up our plates and go to the arcade room and tell the person working there that we're staff kids. He gives us more of the crew cards we used last night!

I put Peaches on top of one of the pinball machines. She's my good luck mascot! I play the best game of pinball I've ever played. I'm feeling so proud of myself, but when my score flashes across the screen, I see that I'm not even in the top one hundred.

The *Wandering Princess* is my new home. Right now I'm getting newbie scores! But I should be able to get to the top of every leaderboard at the arcade. Then I'd become famous, and I'd have enough money to buy Mom her own room onboard the ship so she could live with us too. I see Max's name in the top five scores and frown. Maybe I'll be better at a different game.

I play a few more games and win a stuffed bear for Peaches.

"Don't worry," I tell her. "They'd never stuff real animals."

Simone comes on the loudspeaker again. This time, she's just making an announcement, not telling sad stories. "DJ Ice Man will be playing at the main pool in five minutes. Don't miss the chance to come show us your frosty moves!"

"Caitlin!" Dylan shouts, appearing from behind a car-racing game. "Time to go!"

He's carrying his breakfast leftovers in one hand and has a Slinky prize bouncing in the other.

"Dylan," I say. "You don't have any moves. Frosty or defrosted."

"Doesn't matter," he says. "A real DJ is here! At a real pool party! We can't miss it."

Max and Olivia are carrying food and prizes

too, and their prizes are *way* bigger than my stuffed bear. It makes me feel embarrassed. I shove the bear in my pocket quickly and put Peaches on my shoulder. We head to the pool.

"The main pool is on Floor Number Ten," I say as we get into the elevator.

"Close. It's Floor Number Nine. Don't worry, newbie, you'll learn." Max pushes the button for FLOOR #9. My cheeks get hot. I should have double-checked my journal before I said the floor number. I wish Dylan would slow down! I start to feel nervous. We're doing too many things. This summer was supposed to be about spending time in one place, not running to every place at once!

We set our stuff on lounge chairs next to the biggest pool I've ever seen. For a Florida kid, that's saying something! There are hundreds of green-and-white–striped lounge chairs lining the deck. Pink umbrellas hang overhead. The pool is divided into several sections. There's lap swim-ming, an open swim area, and a place for kids with colorful fountains and a wave pool. I barely get to take it all in before Dylan and Max kick off their flip-flops.

"COWABUNGA!" they yell at the same time as they cannonball into the pool.

"What do you want to do?" Olivia asks.

"I think maybe I just want to sit for a second."

"Me too," Olivia says. "I love sunbathing."

She puts on her sunglasses and lies back on her chair. Then she takes out her sad book. "Ahh, this is the life."

Peaches crawls off my shoulder and munches on her bell peppers. I take a second to think about what I want to do next. From the lounge chairs, I can see that above the giant main pool, there's *another* pool on a deck one floor higher than us. There are three waterslides that start from a ladder by the main pool before twisting overhead, above the upper deck and over the top of the whole ship. They all have steep drops that land back in another section of the main pool. The smallest slide is blue, then there's a yellow tube slide, and then the biggest slide is clear. It twists all around the pool deck, over the top of the upper deck, and there's even a part where it hangs over the ocean before a steep landing in a corner of the main pool. I know what I want to do. What I *need* to do.

"Olivia, will you watch Peaches while I go on the slide?" I ask.

"It would be my honor," Olivia says seriously.

She puts Peaches on her lap. They both look happy and content. I can tell Peaches loves the warm sun and Olivia's soft towel.

"Be right back!" I say. I take a deep breath and walk slowly. My heart beats faster and faster as I get closer to the clear slide—the biggest one on the cruise ship. If I can conquer the biggest slide here, then I can conquer anything. I'll know that I belong onboard the *Wandering Princess*, just like all the other crew members who rode it. Just like Max. If I ride it more times than him, *he'll* become the newbie!

There's a guy wearing red lifeguard swim trunks with a whistle around his neck waiting at the bottom of the slide. He looks around the same age as my cousin who's in college.

"Hey," he says. "You're one of the new staff kids, right? I saw your lizard in the lobby yesterday."

"Yeah! Peaches is my bearded dragon. My dad is the ship doctor."

"Sweet," he says. "Then if you get hurt on the slide, he can take care of you."

"Umm . . . is there a good chance of me getting hurt?"

"Probably not." He shrugs. "You sure you want to ride the clear one though? It's pretty freaky feeling like you're floating with nothing to hold you up. Almost made me barf my first night here."

I gulp. I close my eyes and try to imagine zipping through the slide, laughing and smiling the whole time. I think about how good it'll feel to splash into the cool water at the end. Then I imagine telling Mom and Dad that I rode the biggest, scariest slide on the ship, and now I'm officially a crew kid. But then other *what-if*s start filling my mind.

What if I get flipped around and land in the pool headfirst?

What if I throw up on the clear slide, and everyone down below can see?

What if I don't actually belong on the Wandering Princess?

"Um, maybe I'll start with the blue slide," I say, pointing to the smallest slide. Its cylinder is made of solid blue plastic. No one will be able to see me get sick.

"Smart choice," he says. "Alright, it's your turn. Get up there!"

I put my feet in the slide and push myself down the first dip. The small slide zips me around gently. It's so dark inside the blue plastic, I can't see anything. For a second, I feel disappointed that I didn't get on the clear slide. At least now Max and Dylan can't see that I failed to become a real crew kid. Then the blue slide dips me down, once, then twice—then a third time! I can't help but squeal in delight.

I keep laughing as the waterslide makes its final descent. There's a final little drop, and then— SPLASH! I have just a second to hold my nose before I fly feetfirst into the water at the bottom of the slide. I use my free hand to swim back to the surface and over to the edge of the pool.

Olivia waves to me from her sunbathing chair. I don't think she noticed which slide I came out.

I breathe a sigh of relief, and water comes out my nose. I wipe it away before I get *another* reason to be embarrassed.

"Look, Peaches made a new friend!" Olivia shouts.

"Uhh . . . say what now?" I push myself up over the edge of the pool. Olivia's holding Peaches while she sits next to a tiny white dog with fluffy curly fur.

"I'm sorry," I quickly apologize to the dog's owner, worried that she'll be mad at Peaches and Olivia. "Peaches has never met a dog before . . ."

"Oh, don't apologize!" the woman says. "Look at them. They're in love. I think they want to get married."

They do look like they're in love. Peaches and the dog touch the tips of their noses together.

"This is Pearl," the woman says. "She's a poodle, and she *loves* love."

Pearl rolls over onto her belly. Her tongue slips out the side of her mouth and brushes against Peaches's spiky beard.

"Hi, Pearl," I say, giggling. "I'm Caitlin."

The woman smiles, then says loudly, in a sing-songy voice, "And *I'm* Gigi!"

Gigi is wearing bright red lipstick, blue eye shadow, and three pearl necklaces. She has a ring on every finger, and her dark hair is in a fancy bun on top of her head. Her giant sunglasses are dotted with jewels, and she's wearing a fancy silk robe over her swimsuit.

"Bearded dragons are fascinating creatures, aren't they?" Gigi says. She's talking to me, but she's so loud she might as well be talking to everyone at the pool. "I starred in a play that had a bearded dragon in it once, though we used a stuffed animal, not the real thing. I didn't want any dragon poo getting on my costumes."

I laugh. I like Gigi. And Pearl too.

"Actually, bearded dragons don't always go to the bathroom every day, and Peaches likes to go in her favorite corner in her tank, so she won't poo on our clothes. Unless she's eaten too many blueberries that day. Did you say you were in a play? Are you an actress?"

Gigi sits up straight. "Why, yes, I am! A rather famous one. If you were a generation or two older, you'd have heard of me. But I've been retired for a while."

"That's so cool! I'd love to hear more about your plays. And do you want to know more about a bearded dragon's natural habitat? Let me just make some room to sit down—"

I pick up my plate of leftover breakfast, but when I turn to set it down, I trip over my prize bear. The plate slips out of my hand and lands on Gigi's silk robe with a large *splat*. The smell of waffles and bacon fills my nostrils as the food turns into a huge, gloopy mess.

A person's shadow falls over me. I turn around, and my heart sinks.

It's Simone.

CHAPTER SIX

CRUISE CONTROL

"I am so sorry," Simone says over and over again.

"Caitlin is one of our staff members' children. I'll

talk to her about this. And I'd love to offer you a

free massage."

Gigi looks too shocked to say anything. Pearl licks maple syrup off her knee.

"Come on, Caitlin," Simone says, her hand on my shoulder. "Let's go to my office." I pick up Peaches and turn to follow her.

"Wait!" Gigi cries, but I don't look back. I feel too awful. I wonder what will happen to me if I get kicked off the ship. Will I go home to Mom? Will Dad get kicked off too? So much for having a cruise ship as a home.

Olivia walks beside me. I don't know why she's coming with me—she didn't do anything wrong! Maybe she's just a really good friend. Simone leads us to her office, which is a room off to the side of the main lobby. When we get inside, Max and Dylan are already there, dripping chlorine water all over the floor. They both have their shoulders hunched. I wonder what they did to end up in here.

Simone's office has a wall of shelves filled with ship manuals, a small window looking out over the ocean, and a large desk with a few chairs in front. Olivia and I sit down next to the boys. Simone steps beside my chair. I'm so worried I can hardly breathe. Peaches rubs her bristly beard against my arms, and it makes me feel a little better.

The door to Simone's office opens again. Dad and Chef Benedict walk inside. Dad's wearing scrubs and sunglasses, and Chef Benedict's chef uniform is splattered with chocolate sauce. They both look disappointed. I bet they were really busy, and now we ruined their day too!

"Thanks for joining me, everyone. Kids, no need to look so worried."

"We're not getting kicked off the ship?" I ask.

The corners of Simone's lips turn upward. "Of course not. This is just a reminder to be careful," Simone says. "There are a lot of people on this ship, and I need to be able to count on you all to help keep things calm, not cause chaos."

Dylan nods seriously. "No more cowabungas," he promises.

"And you need to take things slow," Dad says, running his hands through his hair. "No more jam-packed plans."

"I have an idea," Chef Benedict says. "Why don't you all come help me in the kitchen this afternoon? Don't worry, Simone, I'll keep them in line."

"I have no doubt about that," Simone says. "Thanks, everyone, for being so understanding."

"We're really sorry," Dylan says. The rest of us nod in agreement.

Chef Benedict tells us to meet him in the kitchens in two hours, so we have a little time to chill out. Dad walks me and Dylan back to our room, where I put Peaches back in her tank and make sure her heater lights are on. Then I turn on the dehumidifier, which takes all the water out of the air. That's because bearded dragons are from the desert, so even though Peaches loves the hot Florida sun, sometimes it's too humid for her. Sometimes it's too humid for me too. My curls stick to my sweaty face.

I flop down onto my bed, and Dylan flops onto the floor.

"I don't even have the energy to get to the second bunk," he says.

"What happened with your cowabungas?" I ask him.

"Well, after Max and I rode the clear slide—which is *awesome*, by the way. Max says I'm officially a crew kid now. Not a newbie anymore."

My heart sinks. Even Dylan rode the slide.

That means he belongs on the *Wandering Princess*. But I still haven't proved that I'm a crew kid yet. What if the other crew members find out I was too scared to ride, and they send me away? Where will my home be then?

"Well, so after that, Max and I decided to see if we could make a splash as big as the slide when it shoots you out. So we did a double cannonball, and we splashed some guests who were getting manicures. I felt bad."

I sigh. "I got maple syrup all over a former famous actress. I think that's worse."

I wipe my hair from my face and close my eyes. Before I know it, I wake up to a knock on the door. Dylan and I fell asleep! Max and Olivia are here to bring us to the kitchens. I blow Peaches a kiss goodbye. Bearded dragons aren't allowed in the kitchens, which I guess makes sense.

The kitchens are huge. Everything is made out of shiny silver metal—the walls, the giant ovens, the pots and pans hanging from the ceiling, and the long benches where Chef Benedict and the other cooks make the meals.

Chef Benedict gives us each a job. "Some customers think the buffet line is overwhelming. They don't like all the choices. I thought maybe you could make a few ready-to-eat plates for them, Caitlin. What do you think?"

What if I secretly have excellent taste in food, and all the cruise ship guests line up to get the Caitlin Special?

"I'd love to!" I tell Chef Benedict.

I get to work making plates filled with all my favorite foods. One scoop of Chef Benedict's five-cheese macaroni, a taco with pink pickled onions, and a slice of pepperoni pizza, plus three carrots and a piece of lettuce—for the guests' health. After I make the plates, I fold a piece of paper in half and write *Caitlin Special* on one side. I set the plates out on the end of the buffet table and prop up my sign in front. Then I sit behind my table and wait for guests to come get their meals!

Gigi and Pearl are my first customers. Gigi's wearing a new outfit that's not covered in maple syrup. I gulp.

"Caitlin," Gigi says kindly. "I'm sorry about that hubbub earlier. I wanted to tell you that I wasn't upset. In fact, I have a flair for the dramatics. That was quite a scene we made. I loved it!

"And Pearl *loves* maple syrup," she continues. "She loves pepperoni too. Can we have a Caitlin Special?"

I sit up straight and smile. "Thank you. I'm so glad you aren't mad. You can have as many Caitlin Specials as you want!"

"Ooh, these look good," Gigi says, picking up

the single piece of lettuce on her plate. "You know, I always say everything in moderation, especially lettuce."

After I run out of Caitlin Specials, I go to the ship infirmary to help Dad. I bring Peaches with me. She cheers up all of Dad's patients.

A small boy with a scrape on his knee tickles Peaches's beard. "Doesn't she need a diaper or something?" he asks. "What if she poops on your shoulder?"

So many passengers want to know about bearded dragon poo! It is interesting, I guess. "Actually, some adult bearded dragons, like Peaches, only poop once or twice a week," I tell him. "And Peaches always goes in her special corner in her tank. So I don't really have to worry about that."

At the end of the day, I finally feel like I did something good on the ship! It was nice helping people, even if it meant talking about dragon poo. So for the next few days, Dylan, Max, Olivia, and I spend our time helping everyone onboard. I learn the layout of the ship and give people directions, and I only send people to the wrong floor a few times. I meet so many different people—a family of ten who came down from Alaska, a group of friends in their nineties who've been taking cruises together for fifty years, and tons of kids my age who are on summer vacation. I write lots of new questions in my *What If?* journal.

What if Mr. Thomas the accountant is actually an alien with eyes on the back of his head, and that's how he always knows when I'm walking behind him?

What if the clear slide went underwater and a shark swam by? What if the shark ate me and Peaches and we had to live in its belly?

What if a whale swallowed the shark, and me and Peaches and the shark had to live in the whale's belly together? Would we become friends?

What if I got to live on the ship forever, but I was like the wandering princess, haunting everyone and never really having a home?

At the end of every day, I call Mom and tell her everything I've been up to. Helping guests is fun but exhausting! Staying out of trouble is hard work. It might be even more intense than Dylan's strict schedule.

Mom asks me if I'm feeling more at home now that we've been on the ship awhile. I say *yes*, even though I mean *almost*. Even though I have my journal to help, I still get lost more than Dylan. And I haven't ridden the slide yet. I still feel like a newbie. All the crew members talk about it.

"I can't wait for our day off tomorrow," Dylan says with a yawn. He climbs up to his bed and gets under the covers.

"Day off? You mean no work?" I ask.

"Yeah, exactly! Tomorrow the *Wandering Princess* docks on St. Thomas. Dad said almost all of the passengers are planning on getting off the ship, so we get to spend all day relaxing. We can cannonball without worrying about splashing anyone! And we can ride the clear slide again."

My heart sinks. Every time Dylan talks about the slide, I tell him that I loved it. I just don't tell him *which* slide I loved. But tomorrow, I won't be able to hide.

Tomorrow, everyone—including me—will find out whether I'm a real crew kid or not.

CHAPTER SEVEN

STOWAWAYS

Max goes first. He doesn't even hesitate—just throws his whole body onto the clear slide and swooshes away. I hear his screams as he zooms around the twists and turns. Almost all the passengers are at the beach today, which means the crew members get to have a little fun. My stomach isn't having any fun though. I feel like I'm going to throw up before I even get on the slide. I tried to make excuses to not go on—like I said that someone needed to stay with Peaches. But Dylan convinced me that we could just attach her leash to one of the lounge chairs. With no passengers around, it's not like Peaches could get into any trouble. So she's waiting down by the pool for us. And I'm wishing I could disappear.

Olivia and Dylan go next, and then it's just me, standing on the slide platform, trying not to get sick.

"You got this, kid," the lifeguard says to me. It's the same guy who told me that the clear slide almost made him barf. "You've been on the ship for a while now. I know you can handle it. And if you don't want to, just go down the blue slide again. I love that one."

I love that one too, but if I don't go on the clear slide, everyone will know I'm a newbie who doesn't belong on the *Wandering Princess*.

"I'm gonna ride the clear one," I insist.

"Alright, you do you," says the lifeguard.

I take a deep breath and scoot myself onto the clear slide. I hold onto the top of the circular opening and slowly slide my legs forward. I can see right through the slide—beneath my legs is nothing but empty space, all the way down to the pool and the deck below.

What if the slide comes apart and I fall that whole way?

I make up my mind before more *what-ifs* can flood it. I scoot back and get out of the slide. I don't look at the lifeguard, and I don't even get on the blue slide. I'm too embarrassed. I want to go home—but I don't know where that is. I run back down the stairs that connect the tall slides to the pool. I'm halfway down when I hear shouting.

"Peaches!"

"Wait!"

"She's getting away!"

I lean over the stair railing and see Dylan chasing after Peaches. She's dragging her leash behind her—she must have gotten loose somehow. *Oh no.* If I'd just gone down the slide, I'd be down there already! I reach the bottom of the stairs and race after the others. I run past the pool toward the elevator, where Dylan is hunched over, gasping for air.

"What happened?" I cry.

"The knot on her leash came loose. She ran onto the elevator. I don't know what floor it went to."

"Let's split up," Max says. "I'll search the arcade. Dylan and Olivia, go to the dining hall."

"I'll see if she went back to the room," I say, swallowing the lump stuck in my throat.

But when I get back to the room, she's nowhere

to be found. If she didn't want to go to her safe space—her tank—then where could she be? I decide to search one floor at a time. I take the elevator up to the lobby and help desk, but no one's seen Peaches. And the crew member at the help desk gave me a stern look when she heard Peaches was missing. I know this is going to get back to Simone. My heart sinks. Still, I can't give up on Peaches. I head to the second floor.

I've never been to the board game room—Max says it's boring and full of old people. He was right. Even on beach day, there are lots of passengers here, and most of them have gray hair and big glasses.

I run between tables where people are playing

cards and Scrabble, and then I see it—the end of Peaches's leash! I catch up to her as she scuttles beneath an empty table. I crawl underneath and pull her into my arms.

"Peaches, what are you doing? I was so worried about you!"

Peaches's eyes look wide and scared. I know how she feels.

What if Simone kicks Peaches off the ship when she finds out what happened?

What if Peaches never liked being on the Wandering Princess *anyway?*

What if she feels like she doesn't belong and she doesn't have a home anywhere?

"Don't worry, Peaches," I whisper. "We'll make

a home together. Somewhere no one can find us or kick us out or tell us that we're not real crew kids."

I've made a decision.

Peaches and I are going to run away.

"Now, where are you two going?" Gigi's voice calls out. So much for running away. We got caught before we even left the board game room.

But Peaches does happy tippy taps when she sees Pearl, and Pearl rolls onto her back and wags her tail. Gigi and Pearl are our friends. Maybe it's okay to trust them.

"Peaches and I are running away," I admit. "We don't belong on the ship, and we want to find our own home somewhere we can be alone."

"Running away? Ooh, that's so dramatic. I love it. Where should we hide?"

I smile. "You're coming with us?"

"Of course," Gigi says. "I never miss an opportunity to be a stowaway."

I think about someplace we can go where no one will find us. I'm sure Max, Dylan, and Olivia will be busy searching the busiest places—the arcade, cafeteria, and pools.

"Let's go to the library," I decide. "It's only one floor up. I bet no one ever goes there."

We sneak up to the third floor, looking both ways as we round every corner to make sure no one else notices us. But when we have to walk past a hallway lined with shops in order to get to the library, Gigi gets distracted.

"Quick, in here!" she says as we pass a clothing store. "We need disguises."

She buys dark sunglasses for Peaches and Pearl, and a hat and scarf for me.

"This is actually a good idea," I say. I wrap the scarf around my face and tuck my curls into the hat. "No one will recognize me. Is your disguise ready?"

"Yes!" Gigi announces. She comes out of the dressing room in a floor-length, gold-sequined gown.

"That's not a disguise!"

"Sure it is. People will be distracted by my beauty and not recognize me for the person I am. It's a problem I've faced my whole life."

"Let's just go," I say. I cover Peaches's body with the end of my scarf so all you can see is her head covered in huge sunglasses.

We make one more stop in a candy store for stowaway snacks before reaching the library at the end of the shopping hallway. I was right—there's no one else inside. It's a small square room, but the walls are several stories high. They must go all the way to the fifth floor! The entire room is lined with books, and there are ladders along the wall to help you get the books at the top. Peaches and I will never get bored living here. Olivia would love it. I feel a slight pang of guilt as I think about her. She, Dylan, and Max are probably still looking for me and Peaches. The library is cozy and safe, but it feels empty without my friends and family. It doesn't feel like home. I shake the thought away.

"Do you want me to pick you out a book?" I ask Gigi.

"I haven't much time for reading," Gigi says. "That story we hear over the loudspeaker every night is enough for me. And even that would be much more interesting if an actress were doing the reading."

"The story of the wandering princess? I'm not

sure I like that one. It's too sad. I wish the wandering princess had found her home. I don't think I'd like traveling alongside shooting stars. They never get a chance to rest. Do you think she's really stuck up there in the stars?"

"It's just a story," Gigi says kindly. "Even if it's true, it can still change. If you don't like the ending, write a new one! When I was an actress, I rewrote scripts all the time. It got me into trouble a little bit, but the stories were always better after I added a touch of Gigi magic."

My brain starts buzzing with ideas.

What if I added some Caitlin magic to the wandering princess story?

And then I realize—the wandering princess and I aren't that different.

We're both looking for someplace to call home.

If I can change her story, maybe I can change mine too.

CHAPTER EIGHT

CAITLIN MAGIC

Gigi and I hatch a new plan. It involves leaving our hiding spot, but I don't think Peaches will mind. She's having too much fun with Pearl.

When Gigi's watch shows that the passengers

are all back onboard for the night, we head up to the radio tower on the upper deck of Floor #10. That's where Simone makes announcements from the loudspeaker. We get there just in time. She's about to start the wandering princess story that she tells every night. She looks surprised to see us.

"Caitlin! And I see you've found our runaway, Peaches."

"Peaches didn't mean to run away," I say. "She's very sorry. She just got overwhelmed by the ship. Please don't say she has to go."

Gigi gasps in horror. "Simone would never separate Peaches from her love, my Pearl! Especially since I plan to bring a lot of business to this cruise ship this summer."

Simone chuckles. "I wouldn't dream of it, Gigi. Of course Peaches can stay. But she can't be left unattended."

"I promise it won't happen again."

"Well, I know there are some folks worried about her," Simone says. "Is that why you're here? Should I announce that she's been found?"

"Actually," I say, "Gigi and I had another idea. I wrote a new ending for the wandering princess story, and I think Gigi should read it. She's a professional actress, if you didn't know."

"Oh yes, I've heard." Simone laughs. "Sure, why not? You two have at it. I could use a break."

She passes her microphone to Gigi, who erupts in a coughing fit.

"Oh dear," she says in a voice that sounds like a frog choking on one of Peaches's bugs. "I seem to have lost my voice. You'll have to tell the story, Caitlin."

My eyes go wide. "Really? But 3,026 people are listening."

Gigi coughs again and hands the microphone to me. My voice is shaky at first, but it gets stronger as I go on. I tell the story of the wandering princess, using the same script I've heard Simone read every night.

". . . She left the ship, and now she wanders the skies, traveling alongside shooting stars, always looking for a home that can't be found. But her spirit remains here with us, and we remember her journey as we sail the seas together . . ."

As I get to the end of the story, I start to use my own words.

"She is the wandering princess, ruler of the sea. She follows the path of the crashing waves, but she is not lost. Her kingdom is here, with her loyal companions, because home isn't just one place. The princess's home and kingdom are wherever she is surrounded by the people she loves. That includes all of you! Thank you for traveling with the *Wandering Princess*. When you're here, you're home!"

Even from up here in the radio tower, I can hear passengers on the upper deck applauding.

Behind me, Simone and Gigi clap excitedly. The door to the radio tower bursts open—it's Dad and Dylan! And Dad's holding his phone up to me—I see Mom's face on it!

"Surprise!" Mom says. "Your dad video called me as soon as he heard your voice on the loud-speaker. That was amazing!"

I give Mom a virtual air hug before wrapping my arms tight around Dad.

"I'm glad I have a lot of homes," I say. "No matter where I go, I get to be with one of you. And that's awesome."

Mom and Dad smile widely. "We're so proud of you, Caitlin," Dad says.

"When the cruise ship docks, I'll be there to pick you up," Mom promises. "You and Dylan can stay with me for a few weeks."

"About that . . ." I turn to see Simone speaking. "I was actually hoping Caitlin and Dylan might stay onboard the *Wandering Princess* for the rest of the summer. 'The *Wandering Princess*. When you're here, you're home!' That was AMAZING. I'm going to use it as our ship slogan! I think I need you two around as part of my marketing team."

Dad and Mom look at each other, and she nods.

"That's settled, then," Dad says. "You two can stay onboard with me."

"Yes!" Dylan shouts. He pumps his fists in the air. "More time to build some muscle."

"You haven't lifted weights once," I remind him, laughing.

Max and Olivia are waiting for us outside the radio tower.

Olivia hugs me. "That was so good! I loved your story even more than my tragic ones."

Max looks impressed. "I haven't even been in the radio tower. You're definitely not a newbie anymore."

"I'll bring you inside," I say. "IF you tell me what happened to your hair."

He sighs and rubs his bald head. "It had something to do with a whole box of purple hair dye, some silly string, and a rogue razor. But that's ALL I'm saying!"

I cross my arms, not fully satisfied. But I can think of one more thing Max can help me with.

The next day, the sky is clearer than ever, and the waves crash against the ship in a smooth, gentle rhythm. I'm ready. I know I don't need to ride the clear slide to prove that I belong on the *Wandering Princess*, but I still want to conquer my fears. And Max drew me a map of every twist and turn so I'd know what to expect. This time, when I scoot myself onto the clear slide, I don't think about the slide breaking. I know the ship is strong enough to hold me. Instead, I think about Dad and Dylan and Peaches watching me from down below. And off I go.

The slide takes me up and down and all around the ship. I hold my breath as I get closer to the biggest loop on the slide—the one that takes me right over the ship's edge. For a second, I close my eyes. Then I think about how cool it is that *this* is my home, and that I get to live on this ship. I take a deep breath for courage and open my eyes again. I round the corner, and suddenly I can see the blue ocean beneath me. I slide over the white-tipped waves. I'm moving so fast that I can't help but scream.

"AAAAAH! THIS. IS. AWESOME!" I shout.

And I think of one more question to add to my journal.

What if this turns out to be the
BEST SUMMER EVER?

All aboard for Caitlin's next adventure!

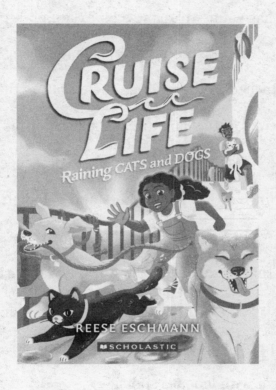

Max, Olivia, and I head to the cruise ship elevator and take it eight floors down to the lobby. The
lobby has white walls and a blue diamond–printed
carpet. There's soothing jazz playing from speak-
ers attached to the ceiling. The elevators that lead
to the rest of the ship are at the back of the lobby.
On the sides there are desks where passengers can
check in with crew members and get their room
keys. And at the front of the lobby, there's a big
ramp that leads out to the dock. A lady in a long
black dress is walking up the ramp. One side of her
giant purse is made of clear plastic. Inside, I can
see a cat with leopard spots!

There are already some other passengers
spread out in the lobby too. My eyes go to a familiar

figure in a hot pink dress covered in jewels. Her hair is in a fancy bun, she's wearing giant purple earrings, and her sunglasses are as big as her face.

"Gigi! What are you doing here?" I ask, running up to give her a hug.

Gigi was my favorite passenger on our first trip of the cruise. She helped me learn how to write my own ending to a story. But Gigi doesn't have a cat, so I don't think she's a member of the Fancy Feline Society of North Carolina. I wonder why she's here.

A yapping sound comes from Gigi's purse. It's her dog, Pearl! Pearl is a little white poodle. She and Peaches are best friends. But even though Pearl is very fancy, she's definitely not a feline.

"I'm a member of the Greater Florida Kennel

Club," Gigi says. "Well, I should get used to saying I *was* a member. This year, I'm running for president of the club. And who wouldn't vote for me? I might as well start calling myself president!"

She twirls in a circle, and the jewels on her dress sparkle.

"I'd vote for you, Gigi!" I say. "And Peaches will be so excited to see Pearl. But what's the Greater Florida Kennel Club? I thought the Fancy Feline Society of North Carolina was coming onboard this week."

"Well, that can't possibly be right," Gigi says. "I put together the Kennel Club cruise itinerary myself. But, well, my eyesight isn't what it used to be. Tell me, that animal in the crate over there . . . is that a dog or a cat?"

"Um, that's definitely a cat . . ." I say, then look to my right. "And over there is a really fluffy dog."

"That lady has an orange tabby cat," Olivia chimes in.

"And that man has a Great Dane that looks as tall as me!" Max says. "Its hair is longer than mine though."

"Uh-oh," I say. "Gigi, I think your cruise got double-booked."

Read about all of Kira's GREAT ideas!

Home for Meow
The Purrfect Show
Reese Eschmann
SCHOLASTIC

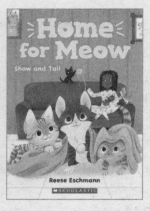

Home for Meow
Show and Tail
Reese Eschmann
SCHOLASTIC

Home for Meow
Kitten Around
Reese Eschmann
SCHOLASTIC

Home for Meow
Two Fur One
Reese Eschmann
SCHOLASTIC

SCHOLASTIC
scholastic.com

HOMEFORMEOW